PENGUIN ARCHIVE

Where Everything is Music

Rumi

1207–1273

A PENGUIN SINCE 1999

Rumi
Where Everything is Music

Translated by Coleman Barks, with John Moyne

PENGUIN ARCHIVE

PENGUIN BOOKS

UK | USA | Canada | Ireland | Australia
India | New Zealand | South Africa

Penguin Books is part of the Penguin Random House group of companies
whose addresses can be found at global.penguinrandomhouse.com

Penguin Random House UK,
One Embassy Gardens, 8 Viaduct Gardens, London SW11 7BW

penguin.co.uk

First published as *The Essential Rumi* in the USA by HarperCollins Publishers 1995
First published in Great Britain in Penguin Books 1999
This selection published in Penguin Classics 2025
006

Translation copyright © Coleman Barks, 1995

The poem titles have been chosen by the translator.

No part of this book may be used or reproduced in any manner for the
purpose of training artificial intelligence technologies or systems. In accordance
with Article 4(3) of the DSM Directive 2019/790, Penguin Random House
expressly reserves this work from the text and data mining exception.

Set in 11.6/15pt Dante MT Std
Typeset by Jouve (UK), Milton Keynes
Printed and bound in Great Britain by Clays Ltd, Elcograf S.p.A.

The authorized representative in the EEA is Penguin Random House Ireland,
Morrison Chambers, 32 Nassau Street, Dublin D02 YH68

A CIP catalogue record for this book is available from the British Library

ISBN: 978–0–241–75236–4

Penguin Random House is committed to a sustainable future
for our business, our readers and our planet. This book is made from
Forest Stewardship Council® certified paper.

Contents

The Milk of Millennia	1
Two Kinds of Intelligence	2
Be Melting Snow	3
A Thirsty Fish	5
Birdwings	7
Joy at Sudden Disappointment	8
'If the beloved is everywhere . . .'	12
Love Dogs	13
In Baghdad, Dreaming of Cairo: In Cairo, Dreaming of Baghdad	15
Story Water	24
Where Are We?	26
'The Friend comes into my body . . .'	28
'There is a light seed grain inside'	28
'Do you think I know what I'm doing?'	28
This World which Is Made of Our Love for Emptiness	29
Craftsmanship and Emptiness	30

The Center of the Fire	35
'Someone who goes with half a loaf of bread . . .'	37
'The mystery does not get clearer by repeating the question . . .'	37
Bismillah	38
Judge a Moth by the Beauty of Its Candle	39
'The morning wind spreads its fresh smell . . .'	40
'Slave, be aware that the Lord . . .'	40
Where Everything is Music	41
The Least Figure	43
'I reach for a piece of wood'	43
Buoyancy	44
I Have Five Things to Say	46
Rough Metaphors	49
The Shape of My Tongue	51
I'm Not Saying This Right	53
A Great Wagon	54
'Today, like every other day . . .'	54
'Out beyond ideas of wrongdoing and rightdoing . . .'	55
'The breeze at dawn has secrets to tell you'	55
'I would love to kiss you'	55

'Daylight, full of small dancing particles . . .'	56
'They try to say what you are . . .'	56
'Come to the orchard in Spring'	56
The Vigil	57
Like This	59
All Rivers at Once	62
The Music	64
'I saw you last night in the gathering'	64
Send the Chaperones Away	65
'When I remember your love . . .'	66
'All our lives we've looked . . .'	67
Water from Your Spring	68
Each Note	69
Music Master	71
'When I am with you, we stay up all night'	72
'The minute I heard my first love story . . .'	72
'We are the mirror as well as the face in it'	72
'I want to hold you close like a lute . . .'	72
Meadowsounds	73
No Room for Form	75
Dying, Laughing	77
A Dove in the Eaves	79

'We have this way of talking . . .'	81
'This piece of food cannot be eaten . . .'	81
'In the slaughterhouse of love . . .'	81
Sublime Generosity	82
Unmarked Boxes	85
Dissolver of Sugar	87
'Pale sunlight . . .'	87
The Fragile Vial	88
Enough Words?	91
My Worst Habit	93
'Don't let your throat tighten . . .'	94
Dervish at the Door	95
Tending Two Shops	98
'Think that you're gliding out . . .'	99
Hallaj	100
Wax	102
Of Being Woven	103
Elephant in the Dark	105
The Waterwheel	107
This We Have Now	108
The Seed Market	110
The Worm's Waking	112

The Milk of Millennia

I am part of the load
not rightly balanced.
I drop off in the grass,
like the old cave-sleepers, to browse
wherever I fall.

For hundreds of thousands of years I have been dust
    grains
floating and flying in the will of the air,
often forgetting ever being
in that state, but in sleep
I migrate back. I spring loose
from the four-branched, time-and-space cross,
this waiting room.

I walk into a huge pasture.
I nurse the milk of millennia.

Everyone does this in different ways.
Knowing that conscious decisions
and personal memory
are much too small a place to live,
every human being streams at night
into the loving nowhere, or during the day,
in some absorbing work.

Two Kinds of Intelligence

There are two kinds of intelligence: one acquired,
as a child in school memorizes facts and concepts
from books and from what the teacher says,
collecting information from the traditional sciences
as well as from the new sciences.

With such intelligence you rise in the world.
You get ranked ahead or behind others
in regard to your competence in retaining
information. You stroll with this intelligence
in and out of fields of knowledge, getting always
    more
marks on your preserving tablets.

There is another kind of tablet, one
already completed and preserved inside you.
A spring overflowing its springbox. A freshness
in the center of the chest. This other intelligence
does not turn yellow or stagnate. It's fluid,
and it doesn't move from outside to inside
through the conduits of plumbing-learning.

This second knowing is a fountainhead
from within you, moving out.

Be Melting Snow

Totally conscious, and apropos of nothing, you come
    to see me.
Is someone here? I ask.
The moon. The full moon is inside your house.

My friends and I go running out into the street.
I'm in here, comes a voice from the house, but we
    aren't listening.
We're looking up at the sky.
My pet nightingale sobs like a drunk in the garden.
Ringdoves scatter with small cries, *Where, Where*.
It's midnight. The whole neighborhood is up and out
in the street thinking, *The cat burglar has come back*.
The actual thief is there too, saying out loud,
Yes, the cat burglar is somewhere in this crowd.
No one pays attention.

Lo, I am with you always means when you look for God,
God is in the look of your eyes,
in the thought of looking, nearer to you than your self,
or things that have happened to you.
There's no need to go outside.

Be melting snow.
Wash yourself of yourself.

A white flower grows in the quietness.
Let your tongue become that flower.

A Thirsty Fish

I don't get tired of you. Don't grow weary
of being compassionate toward me!

All this thirst equipment
must surely be *tired* of me,
the water jar, the water carrier.

I have a thirsty fish in me
that can never find enough
of what it's thirsty for!

Show me the way to the ocean!
Break these half-measures,
these small containers.

All this fantasy
and grief.

Let my house be drowned in the wave
that rose last night out of the courtyard
hidden in the center of my chest.

Joseph fell like the moon into my well.
The harvest I expected was washed away.
But no matter.

A fire has risen above my tombstone hat.
I don't want learning, or dignity,
or respectability.

I want this music and this dawn
and the warmth of your cheek against mine.

The grief-armies assemble,
but I'm not going with them.

This is how it always is
when I finish a poem.

A great silence overcomes me,
and I wonder why I ever thought
to use language.

Birdwings

Your grief for what you've lost lifts a mirror
up to where you're bravely working.

Expecting the worst, you look, and instead,
here's the joyful face you've been wanting to see.

Your hand opens and closes and opens and closes.
If it were always a fist or always stretched open,
you would be paralyzed.

Your deepest presence is in every small contracting
and expanding,
the two as beautifully balanced and coordinated
as birdwings.

Joy at Sudden Disappointment

Whatever comes, comes from a need,
a sore distress, a hurting want.

Mary's pain made the baby Jesus.
Her womb opened its lips
and spoke the Word.

Every part of you has a secret language.
Your hands and your feet say what you've done.

And every need brings in what's needed.
Pain bears its cure like a child.

Having nothing produces provisions.
Ask a difficult question,
and the marvelous answer appears.

Build a ship, and there'll be water
to float it. The tender-throated
infant cries and milk drips
from the mother's breast.

Be thirsty for the ultimate water,
and then be ready for what will
come pouring from the spring.

A village woman once was walking by Muhammad.
She thought he was just an ordinary illiterate.
She didn't believe that he was a prophet.

She was carrying a two-month-old baby.
As she came near Muhammad, the baby turned
and said, 'Peace be with you, Messenger of God.'

The mother cried out, surprised and angry,
'What are you saying,
and how can you suddenly talk!'

The child replied, 'God taught me first,
and then Gabriel.'
      'Who is this Gabriel?
I don't see anyone.'
       'He is above your head,
Mother. Turn around. He has been telling me
many things.'
      'Do you really see him?'
           'Yes.
He is continually delivering me from this
degraded state into sublimity.'

Muhammad then asked the child,
'What is your name?'

'Abdul Aziz, the servant of God, but this family
thinks I am concerned with world-energies.
I am as free of that as the truth of your prophecy is.'

So the little one spoke, and the mother
took in a fragrance that let her surrender
to that state.
              When God gives this knowing,
inanimate stones, plants, animals, everything,
fills with unfolding significance.

The fish and the birds become protectors.
Remember the incident of Muhammad and the eagle.

It happened that as he was listening
to this inspired baby, he heard a voice
calling him to prayer. He asked for water
to perform ablutions. He washed his hands
and feet, and just as he reached for his boot,

an eagle snatched it away! The boot turned upsidedown
as it lifted, and a poisonous snake dropped out.

The eagle circled and brought the boot back,
saying, 'My helpless reverence for you
made this necessary. Anyone who acts

this presumptuously for a legalistic reason
should be punished!'

                Muhammad thanked the eagle,
and said, 'What I thought was rudeness
was really love. You took away my grief,
and I was grieved! God has shown me everything,
but at that moment I was preoccupied within myself.'
The eagle,
       'But chosen one, any clarity I have
comes from you!'
             This spreading radiance
of a True Human Being has great importance.

Look carefully around you and recognize
the luminosity of souls. Sit beside those
who draw you to that.
             Learn from this eagle story
that when misfortune comes, you must quickly praise.

Others may be saying, *Oh no*, but you
will be opening out like a rose
losing itself petal by petal.

Someone once asked a great sheikh
what sufism was.
          'The feeling of joy
when sudden disappointment comes.'

The eagle carries off Muhammad's boot
and saves him from snakebite.

Don't grieve for what doesn't come.
Some things that don't happen
keep disasters from happening.

*

If the beloved is everywhere,
the lover is a veil,

but when living itself becomes
the Friend, lovers disappear.

Love Dogs

One night a man was crying,
                        Allah! Allah!
His lips grew sweet with the praising,
until a cynic said,
               'So! I have heard you
calling out, but have you ever
gotten any response?'

The man had no answer to that.
He quit praying and fell into a confused sleep.

He dreamed he saw Khidr, the guide of souls,
in a thick, green foliage.
                        'Why did you stop praising?'
'Because I've never heard anything back.'
                              'This longing
you express *is* the return message.'

The grief you cry out from
draws you toward union.

Your pure sadness
that wants help
is the secret cup.

Listen to the moan of a dog for its master.
That whining is the connection.

There are love dogs
no one knows the names of.

Give your life
to be one of them.

In Baghdad, Dreaming of Cairo: In Cairo, Dreaming of Baghdad

No more muffled drums!
Uncover the drumheads!

Plant your flag in an open field!
No more timid peeking around.

Either you see the beloved,
or you lose your head!

If your throat's not ready for that wine, cut it!
If your eyes don't want the fullness of union,
let them turn white with disease.

Either this deep desire of mine
will be found on this journey,
or when I get back home!

It may be that the satisfaction I need
depends on my going away, so that when I've gone
and come back, I'll find it at home.

I will search for the Friend with all my passion
and all my energy, until I learn
that I don't need to search.

The real truth of existence is sealed,
until after many twists and turns of the road.

As in the algebraical method of 'the two errors',
the correct answer comes only after two substitutions,
after two mistakes. Then the seeker says,

'If I had known the real way it was,
I would have stopped all the looking around.'

But that knowing depends
on the time spent looking!

Just as the sheikh's debt could not be paid
until the boy's weeping, the story we told in Book II.

You fear losing a certain eminent position.
You hope to gain something from that, but it comes
from elsewhere. Existence does this switching trick,
giving you hope from one source, then
satisfaction from another.
                        It keeps you bewildered
and wondering, and lets your trust in the unseen
   grow.

You think to make your living from tailoring,
but then somehow money comes in
through goldsmithing,
which had never entered your mind.

I don't know whether the union I want will come
through my effort, or my giving up effort,
or from something completely separate
from anything I do or don't do.

I wait and fidget and flop about
as a decapitated chicken does, knowing that
the vital spirit has to escape this body
eventually, somehow!

This desire will find an opening.

There was once a man
who inherited a lot of money and land.

But he squandered it all too quickly. Those who inherit
wealth don't know what work it took to get it.

In the same way, we don't know the value of our souls,
which were given to us for nothing!

So the man was left alone without provisions,
an owl in the desert.

                The Prophet has said
that a true seeker must be completely empty like a lute
to make the sweet music of *Lord, Lord*.

When the emptiness starts to get filled with
    something,
the one who plays the lute puts it down
and picks up another.

There is nothing more subtle and delightful
than to make that music.
                Stay empty and held
between those fingers, where *where*
gets drunk with nowhere.
                This man was empty,
and the tears came. His habitual stubbornness
dissolved. This is the way with many seekers.
They moan in prayer, and the perfumed smoke of that
floats into heaven, and the angels say, 'Answer
this prayer. This worshiper has only you
and nothing else to depend on. Why do you go first
to the prayers of those less devoted?'
                God says,
'By deferring my generosity I am helping him.
His need dragged him by the hair into my presence.
If I satisfy that, he'll go back to being absorbed

in some idle amusement. Listen how passionate he is!
That torn-open cry is the way he should live.'

Nightingales are put in cages
because their songs give pleasure.
Whoever heard of keeping a crow?

When two people, one decrepit and the other young
and handsome, come into a bakery where the baker
is an admirer of young men, and both of them
ask for bread, the baker will immediately
give what he has on hand to the old man.

But to the other he will say, 'Sit down and wait awhile.
There's fresh bread baking in the house. Almost ready!'

And when the hot bread is brought, the baker will say,
'Don't leave. The halvah is coming!'

So he finds ways of detaining the young man with,
'Ah, there's something important I want to tell you
    about.
Stay. I'll be back in a moment. Something very
    important!'

This is how it is when true devotees
suffer disappointment
in the good they want to do,
or the bad they want to avoid.

So this man with nothing, who had inherited
    everything
and squandered it, kept weeping, *Lord, Lord!*

Finally in a dream he heard a voice, 'Your wealth
is in Cairo. Go there to such and such a spot
and dig, and you'll find what you need.'

So he left on the long journey,
and when he saw the towers of Cairo,
he felt his back grow warm with new courage.

But Cairo is a large city,
and before he could find the spot,
he had to wander about.

He had no money, of course, so he begged
among the townspeople, but he felt ashamed doing
    that.
He decided, 'I will go out at night
and call like the night-mendicants that people
throw coins into the street for.'
                        Shame and dignity and hunger
were pushing him forward and backward and
    sideways!

Suddenly, he was seized by the night patrol.
It so happened that many had been robbed recently
in Cairo at night, and the caliph had told the police

to assume that anyone out roaming after dark
was a thief.

                It's best not to let offenders go unpunished.
Then they poison the whole body of society. Cut off
the snakebitten finger! Don't be sympathetic
with thieves. Consider instead
the public suffering. In those days
robbers were expert, and numerous!

So the night patrol grabbed the man.
                                     'Wait!
I can explain!'
            'Tell me.'
                        'I am not a criminal.
I am new to Cairo. I live in Baghdad.' He told the story
of his dream and the buried treasure,
and he was so believable in the telling that
the night patrolman began to cry. Always,
the fragrance of truth has that effect.
                                     Passion
can restore healing power, and prune the weary boughs
to new life. The energy of passion is everything!

There are fake satisfactions that simulate passion.
They taste cold and delicious,
but they just distract you and prevent you
from the search. They say,
                              'I will relieve your passion.
Take me. Take me!'

Run from false remedies
that dilute your energy. Keep it rich and musky.

The night patrol said, 'I know you're not a thief.
You're a good man, but you're kind of a fool.
I've had that dream before.

                        I was told, in my dream,
that there was a treasure for me in Baghdad,
buried in a certain quarter of the city
on such and such a street.'

                        The name of the street
that he said was where this man lived!

                        'And the dream-
voice told me, "It's in So-and-so's house.
Go there and get it!"'

                        Without knowing,
he had described the exact house,
and mentioned this man's name!

                        'But I didn't do
what the dream said to do, and look at you,
who did, wandering the world, fatigued,
and begging in the streets!'

                        So it came quietly
to the seeker, though he didn't say it out loud,
'What I'm longing for lived in my house in Baghdad!'

He filled with joy. He breathed continuous praise.
Finally he said,
> 'The water of life is here.
I'm drinking it. But I had to come
this long way to know it!'

Story Water

A story is like water
that you heat for your bath.

It takes messages between the fire
and your skin. It lets them meet,
and it cleans you!

Very few can sit down
in the middle of the fire itself
like a salamander or Abraham.
We need intermediaries.

A feeling of fullness comes,
but usually it takes some bread
to bring it.

Beauty surrounds us,
but usually we need to be walking
in a garden to know it.

The body itself is a screen
to shield and partially reveal
the light that's blazing
inside your presence.

Water, stories, the body,
all the things we do, are mediums
that hide and show what's hidden.

Study them,
and enjoy this being washed
with a secret we sometimes know,
and then not.

Where Are We?

An invisible bird flies over,
but casts a quick shadow.

What is the body? That shadow of a shadow
of your love, that somehow contains
the entire universe.

A man sleeps heavily,
though something blazes in him like the sun,
like a magnificent fringe sewn up under the hem.

He turns under the covers.
Any image is a lie:

> A clear red stone tastes sweet.

> You kiss a beautiful mouth, and a key
> turns in the lock of your fear.

> A spoken sentence sharpens to a fine edge.

> A mother dove looks for her nest,
> asking where, *ku?* Where, *ku?*

Where the lion lies down.
Where any man or woman goes to cry.
Where the sick go when they hope to get well.

Where a wind lifts that helps with winnowing,
and, the same moment, sends a ship on its way.

Where anyone says *Only God Is Real*.
Ya Hu! Where beyond *where*.

A bright weaver's shuttle flashes back and forth,
east-west, *Where-are-we? Ma ku? Maku,*
like the sun saying *Where are we?*
as it weaves with the asking.

*

The Friend comes into my body
looking for the center, unable
to find it, draws a blade,
strikes anywhere.

*

There is a light seed grain inside.
You fill it with yourself, or it dies.

I'm caught in this curling energy! Your hair!
Whoever's calm and sensible is insane!

*

Do you think I know what I'm doing?
That for one breath or half-breath I belong to
     myself?
As much as a pen knows what it's writing,
or the ball can guess where it's going next.

This World which Is Made of Our Love for Emptiness

Praise to the emptiness that blanks out existence.
    Existence:
this place made from our love for that emptiness!
Yet somehow comes emptiness,
this existence goes.
Praise to that happening, over and over!

For years I pulled my own existence out of emptiness.
Then one swoop, one swing of the arm,
that work is over.
Free of who I was, free of presence, free of
dangerous fear, hope,
free of mountainous wanting.

The here-and-now mountain is a tiny piece of a piece
of straw
blown off into emptiness.

These words I'm saying so much begin to lose
    meaning:
existence, emptiness, mountain, straw: words
and what they try to say swept
out the window, down the slant of the roof.

Craftsmanship and Emptiness

I've said before that every craftsman
searches for what's not there
to practice his craft.

A builder looks for the rotten hole
where the roof caved in. A water carrier
picks the empty pot. A carpenter
stops at the house with no door.

Workers rush toward some hint
of emptiness, which they then
start to fill. Their hope, though,
is for emptiness, so don't think
you must avoid it. It contains
what you need!

                      Dear soul, if you were not friends
with the vast nothing inside,
why would you always be casting your net
into it, and waiting so patiently?

This invisible ocean has given you such abundance,
but still you call it 'death',
that which provides you sustenance and work.

God has allowed some magical reversal to occur,
so that you see the scorpion pit
as an object of desire,
and all the beautiful expanse around it
as dangerous and swarming with snakes.

This is how strange your fear of death
and emptiness is, and how perverse
the attachment to what you want.

Now that you've heard me
on your misapprehensions, dear friend,
listen to Attar's story on the same subject.

He strung the pearls of this
about King Mahmud, how among the spoils
of his Indian campaign there was a Hindu boy,
whom he adopted as a son. He educated
and provided royally for the boy
and later made him vice-regent, seated
on a gold throne beside himself.

One day he found the young man weeping.
'Why are you crying? You're the companion
of an emperor! The entire nation is ranged out
before you like stars that you can command!'

The young man replied, 'I am remembering
my mother and my father, and how they
scared me as a child with threats of you!
"Uh-oh, he's headed for King Mahmud's court!
Nothing could be more hellish!" Where are they now
when they should see me sitting here?'

This incident is about your fear of changing.
You are the Hindu boy. *Mahmud*, which means,
Praise to the End, is the spirit's
poverty, or emptiness.

The mother and father are your attachment
to beliefs and bloodties
and desires and comforting habits.

Don't listen to them!
They seem to protect,
but they imprison.

They are your worst enemies.
They make you afraid
of living in emptiness.

Some day you'll weep tears of delight in that court,
remembering your mistaken parents!

Know that your body nurtures the spirit,
helps it grow, and then gives it wrong advice.

The body becomes, eventually, like a vest
of chainmail in peaceful years,
too hot in summer and too cold in winter.

But the body's desires, in another way, are like
an unpredictable associate, whom you must be
patient with. And that companion is helpful,
because patience expands your capacity
to love and feel peace.

The patience of a rose close to a thorn
keeps it fragrant. It's patience that gives milk
to the male camel still nursing in its third year,
and patience is what the prophets show to us.

The beauty of careful sewing on a shirt
is the patience it contains.

Friendship and loyalty have patience
as the strength of their connections.

Feeling lonely and ignoble indicates
that you haven't been patient.

Be with those who mix with God
as honey blends with milk, and say,

'Anything that comes and goes,
rises and sets,
is not what I love.'

Live in the one who created the prophets,
else you'll be like a caravan fire left
to flare itself out alone beside the road.

The Center of the Fire

No more wine for me!
I'm past delighting in the thick red
and the clear white.

I'm thirsty for my own blood
as it moves into a field of action.

Draw the keenest blade you have
and strike, until the head circles
about the body.

Make a mountain of skulls like that.
Split me apart.

Don't stop at the mouth!
Don't listen to anything I say.
I must enter the center of the fire.

Fire is my child
but I must be consumed
and become fire.

Why is there crackling and smoke?
Because the firewood and the flames
are still talking:

                'You are too dense. Go away!'
'You are too wavering. I have solid form.'

In the blackness those two friends keep arguing.
Like a wanderer with no face.
Like the most powerful bird in existence
sitting on its perch, refusing to move.

What can I say to someone so curled up with wanting,
so constricted in his love?

Break your pitcher against a rock.
We don't need any longer
to haul pieces of the ocean around.

We must drown, away from heroism,
and descriptions of heroism.

Like a pure spirit lying down, pulling
its body over it, like a bride her husband
for a cover to keep her warm.

*

Someone who goes with half a loaf of bread
to a small place that fits like a nest around him,
someone who wants no more, who's not himself
longed for by anyone else,

He is a letter to everyone. You open it.
It says, *Live*.

*

The mystery does not get clearer by repeating the
    question,
nor is it bought with going to amazing places.

Until you've kept your eyes
and your wanting still for fifty years,
you don't begin to cross over from confusion.

Bismillah

It's a habit of yours to walk slowly.
You hold a grudge for years.
With such heaviness, how can you be modest?
With such attachments, do you expect to arrive
 anywhere?

Be wide as the air to learn a secret.
Right now you're equal portions clay
and water, thick mud.

Abraham learned how the sun and moon and the
 stars all set.
He said, *No longer will I try to assign partners for God.*

You are so weak. Give up to grace.
The ocean takes care of each wave
till it gets to shore.
You need more help than you know.
You're trying to live your life in open scaffolding.
Say Bismillah, *In the name of God*,
as the priest does with a knife when he offers an animal.

Bismillah your old self
to find your real name.

Judge a Moth by the Beauty of Its Candle

You are the king's son.
Why do you close yourself up?
Become a lover.

Don't aspire to be a general
or a minister of state.

One is a boredom for you,
the other a disgrace.

You've been a picture on a bathhouse wall
long enough. No one recognizes you here, do they?

God's lion disguised as a human being!
I saw that and put down the book
I was studying, Hariri's *Maqamat*.

There is no early and late for us.
The only way to measure a lover
is by the grandeur of the beloved.

Judge a moth by the beauty of its candle.

Shams is invisible because he is inside sight.
He is the intelligent essence
of what is everywhere at once, seeing.

*

The morning wind spreads its fresh smell.
We must get up and take that in,
that wind that lets us live.
Breathe before it's gone.

*

Slave, be aware that the Lord
of all the East is here.

A flickering storm cloud
shows his lightnings to you!

Your words are guesswork.
He speaks from experience.
There's a huge difference.

Where Everything is Music

Don't worry about saving these songs!
And if one of our instruments breaks,
it doesn't matter.

We have fallen into the place
where everything is music.

The strumming and the flute notes
rise into the atmosphere,
and even if the whole world's harp
should burn up, there will still be
hidden instruments playing.

So the candle flickers and goes out.
We have a piece of flint, and a spark.

This singing art is sea foam.
The graceful movements come from a pearl
somewhere on the ocean floor.

Poems reach up like spindrift and the edge
of driftwood along the beach, wanting!

They derive
from a slow and powerful root
that we can't see.

Stop the words now.
Open the window in the center of your chest,
and let the spirits fly in and out.

The Least Figure

I tried to think of some way
to let my face become yours.

'Could I whisper in your ear
a dream I've had? You're the only one
I've told this to.'

You tilt your head, laughing,
as if, 'I know the trick you're hatching,
but go ahead.'

I am an image you stitch with gold thread
on a tapestry, the least figure,
a playful addition.

But nothing you work on is dull.
I am part of the beauty.

*

I reach for a piece of wood. It turns into a lute.
I do some meanness. It turns out helpful.
I say one must not travel during the holy month.
Then I start out and wonderful things happen.

Buoyancy

Love has taken away my practices
and filled me with poetry.

I tried to keep quietly repeating,
No strength but yours,
but I couldn't.

I had to clap and sing.
I used to be respectable and chaste and stable,
but who can stand in this strong wind
and remember those things?

A mountain keeps an echo deep inside itself.
That's how I hold your voice.

I am scrap wood thrown in your fire,
and quickly reduced to smoke.

I saw you and became empty.
This emptiness, more beautiful than existence,
it obliterates existence, and yet when it comes,
existence thrives and creates more existence!

The sky is blue. The world is a blind man
squatting on the road.

But whoever sees your emptiness
sees beyond blue and beyond the blind man.

A great soul hides like Muhammad, or Jesus,
moving through a crowd in a city
where no one knows him.

To praise is to praise
how one surrenders
to the emptiness.

To praise the sun is to praise your own eyes.
Praise, the ocean. What we say, a little ship.

So the sea-journey goes on, and who knows where!
Just to be held by the ocean is the best luck
we could have. It's a total waking up!

Why should we grieve that we've been sleeping?
It doesn't matter how long we've been unconscious.

We're groggy, but let the guilt go.
Feel the motions of tenderness
around you, the buoyancy.

I Have Five Things to Say

The wakened lover speaks directly to the beloved,
'You are the sky my spirit circles in,
the love inside love, the resurrection-place.

Let this window be your ear.
I have lost consciousness many times
with longing for your listening silence,
and your life-quickening smile.

You give attention to the smallest matters,
my suspicious doubts, and to the greatest.

You know my coins are counterfeit,
but you accept them anyway,
my impudence and my pretending!

I have five things to say,
five fingers to give
into your grace.

First, when I was apart from you,
    this world did not exist,
        nor any other.

Second, whatever I was looking for
> was always you.

Third, why did I ever learn to count to three?

Fourth, my cornfield is burning!

Fifth, this finger stands for Rabia,
> and this is for someone else.
> > Is there a difference?

Are these words or tears?
Is weeping speech?
What shall I do, my love?'

So he speaks, and everyone around
begins to cry with him, laughing crazily,
moaning in the spreading union
of lover and beloved.

This is the true religion. All others
are thrown-away bandages beside it.

This is the *sema* of slavery and mastery
dancing together. This is not-being.

Neither words, nor any natural fact
can express this.

I know these dancers.
Day and night I sing their songs
in this phenomenal cage.

My soul, don't try to answer now!
Find a friend, and hide.
But what can stay hidden?
Love's secret is always lifting its head
out from under the covers,
'Here I am!'

Rough Metaphors

Someone said, 'there is no dervish, or if there is a dervish,
 that dervish is not there.'

Look at a candle flame in bright noon sunlight.
 If you put cotton next to it, the cotton will burn,
  but its light has become completely mixed
   with the sun.

That candlelight you can't find   is what's left of a dervish.

If you sprinkle one ounce of vinegar over
 two hundred tons of sugar,
  no one will ever taste the vinegar.

A deer faints in the paws of a lion. The deer becomes
 another glazed expression on the face of the lion.

These are rough metaphors for what happens to the lover.

There's no one more openly irreverent than a lover.
    He, or she,
        jumps up on the scale opposite eternity
            and claims to balance it.

And no one more secretly reverent.

A grammar lesson: 'The lover died.'
    'Lover' is subject and agent, but that can't be!
        The 'lover' is defunct.

Only grammatically is the dervish-lover a doer.

In reality, with he or she so overcome,
    so dissolved into love,
        all qualities of doingness
            disappear.

The Shape of My Tongue

This mirror inside me shows . . .
I can't say what, but I can't not know!

I run from body. I run from spirit.
I do not belong anywhere.

I'm not alive!
You smell the decay?

You talk about my craziness.
Listen rather to the honed-blade sanity I say.

This gourd head on top of a dervish robe,
do I look like someone you know?

This dipper gourd full of liquid,
upsidedown and not spilling a drop!

Or if it spills, it drops into God
and rounds into pearls.

I form a cloud over that ocean
and gather spillings.

When Shams is here,
I rain.

After a day or two, lilies sprout,
the shape of my tongue.

I'm Not Saying This Right

You bind me, and I tear away in a rage to open out
into air, a round brightness, a candlepoint,
all reason, all love.

This confusing joy, your doing,
this hangover, your tender thorn.

You turn to look, I turn.
I'm not saying this right.

I am a jailed crazy who ties up spirit-women.
I am Solomon.

What goes comes back. Come back.
We never left each other.

A disbeliever hides disbelief,
but I will say his secret.

More and more awake, getting up at night,
spinning and falling with love for Shams.

A Great Wagon

When I see your face, the stones start spinning!
You appear; all studying wanders.
I lose my place.

Water turns pearly.
Fire dies down and doesn't destroy.

In your presence I don't want what I thought
I wanted, those three little hanging lamps.

Inside your face the ancient manuscripts
seem like rusty mirrors.

You breathe; new shapes appear,
and the music of a desire as widespread
as Spring begins to move
like a great wagon.
                        Drive slowly.
Some of us walking alongside
are lame!

★

Today, like every other day, we wake up empty
and frightened. Don't open the door to the study
and begin reading. Take down a musical instrument.

Let the beauty we love be what we do.
There are hundreds of ways to kneel and kiss the
    ground.

★

Out beyond ideas of wrongdoing and rightdoing,
there is a field. I'll meet you there.

When the soul lies down in that grass,
the world is too full to talk about.
Ideas, language, even the phrase *each other*
doesn't make any sense.

★

The breeze at dawn has secrets to tell you.
                Don't go back to sleep.
You must ask for what you really want.
                Don't go back to sleep.
People are going back and forth across the doorsill
                where the two worlds touch.
The door is round and open.
                Don't go back to sleep.

★

I would love to kiss you.
The price of kissing is your life.

Now my loving is running toward my life shouting,
What a bargain, let's buy it.

*

Daylight, full of small dancing particles
and the one great turning, our souls
are dancing with you, without feet, they dance.
Can you see them when I whisper in your ear?

*

They try to say what you are, spiritual or sexual?
They wonder about Solomon and all his wives.

In the body of the world, they say, there is a soul
and you are that.

But we have ways within each other
that will never be said by anyone.

*

Come to the orchard in Spring.
There is light and wine, and sweethearts
      in the pomegranate flowers.

If you do not come, these do not matter.
If you do come, these do not matter.

The Vigil

Don't go to sleep one night.
What you most want will come to you then.
Warmed by a sun inside, you'll see wonders.

Tonight, don't put your head down.
Be tough, and strength will come.
That which adoration adores
appears at night. Those asleep
may miss it. One night Moses stayed awake
and asked, and saw a light in a tree.

Then he walked at night for ten years,
until finally he saw the whole tree
illuminated. Muhammad rode his horse
through the nightsky. The day is for work.
The night for love. Don't let someone
bewitch you. Some people sleep at night.

But not lovers. They sit in the dark
and talk to God, who told David,
*Those who sleep all night every night
and claim to be connected to us, they lie.*

Lovers can't sleep when they feel the privacy
of the beloved all around them. Someone
who's thirsty may sleep for a little while,
but he or she will dream of water, a full jar
beside a creek, or the spiritual water you get
from another person. All night, listen
to the conversation. Stay up.
This moment is all there is.

Death will take it away soon enough.
You'll be gone, and this earth will be left
without a sweetheart, nothing but weeds
growing inside thorns.

I'm through. Read the rest of this poem
in the dark tonight.
                      Do I have a head? And feet?

Shams, so loved by Tabrizians, I close my lips.
I wait for you to come and open them.

Like This

If anyone asks you
how the perfect satisfaction
of all our sexual wanting
will look, lift your face
and say,
> *Like this.*

When someone mentions the gracefulness
of the nightsky, climb up on the roof
and dance and say,
> *Like this?*

If anyone wants to know what 'spirit' is,
or what 'God's fragrance' means,
lean your head toward him or her.
Keep your face there close.
> *Like this.*

When someone quotes the old poetic image
about clouds gradually uncovering the moon,
slowly loosen knot by knot the strings
of your robe.
> *Like this?*

If anyone wonders how Jesus raised the dead,
don't try to explain the miracle.
Kiss me on the lips.
> *Like this. Like this.*

When someone asks what it means
to 'die for love', point
> *here.*

If someone asks how tall I am, frown
and measure with your fingers the space
between the creases on your forehead.
> *This tall.*

The soul sometimes leaves the body, then returns.
When someone doesn't believe that,
walk back into my house.
> *Like this.*

When lovers moan,
they're telling our story.
> *Like this.*

I am a sky where spirits live.
Stare into this deepening blue,
while the breeze says a secret.
> *Like this.*

When someone asks what there is to do,
light the candle in his hand.
>				*Like this.*

How did Joseph's scent come to Jacob?
>				*Huuuuu.*

How did Jacob's sight return?
>				*Huuuu.*

A little wind cleans the eyes.
>				*Like this.*

When Shams comes back from Tabriz,
he'll put just his head around the edge
of the door to surprise us.
>				*Like this.*

All Rivers at Once

Don't unstring the bow.
I am your four-feathered arrow
that has not been used yet.

I am a strong knifeblade word,
not some *if* or *maybe*,
dissolving in air.

I am sunlight slicing the dark.
Who made this night?
A forge deep in the earth-mud.

What is the body?
Endurance.

What is love?
Gratitude.

What is hidden
in our chests?
Laughter.

What else?
Compassion.

Let the beloved be a hat pulled down firmly on my head.
Or drawstrings pulled and tied around my chest.

Someone asks, How does love have hands and feet?
Love is the sprouting bed for hands and feet!

Your father and mother were playing love games.
They came together, and you appeared!

Don't ask what love can make or do!
Look at the colors of the world.

The riverwater moving in all rivers at once.
The truth that lives in Shams' face.

The Music

For sixty years I have been forgetful,
every minute, but not for a second
has this flowing toward me stopped or slowed.
I deserve nothing. Today I recognize
that I am the guest the mystics talk about.
I play this living music for my host.
Everything today is for the host.

★

I saw you last night in the gathering,
but could not take you openly in my arms,

so I put my lips next to your cheek,
pretending to talk privately.

Send the Chaperones Away

Inside me a hundred beings
are putting their fingers to their lips and saying,
'That's enough for now. Shhhhh.' Silence
is an ocean. Speech is a river.

When the ocean is searching for you, don't walk
to the language-river. Listen to the ocean,
and bring your talky business
to an end.

Traditional words are just babbling
in that presence, and babbling is a substitute
for sight. When you sit down beside your beloved,
send the chaperones away, the old women
who brought you together.

When you are mature and with your love,
the love letters and matchmakers
seem irritating.
                You might read those letters,
but only to teach beginners about love. One who sees
grows silent. When you're with one of those,
be still and quiet, unless he asks you
to talk. Then draw the words out

as I do this poem with Husam,
the radiance of God.
                      I try to stop talking,
but he makes me continue. Husam, if you are in
the vision, why do you want me to say *words*?

Maybe it's like the poet Abu Nuwas,
who said in Arabic,
                Pour me some wine,
and talk to me about the wine.
                      The cup is at my mouth
but my ear interrupts,
                      'I want some.'
O ear, what you get is the heat.
You turn red with this wine.
                      But the ear says,
'I want more than that!'

                      *

When I remember your love,
I weep, and when I hear people
talking of you,
                    something in my chest,
where nothing much happens now,
moves as in sleep.

★

All our lives we've looked
into each other's faces.
That was the case today too.

How do we keep our love-secret?
We speak from brow to brow
and hear with our eyes.

Water from Your Spring

What was in that candle's light
that opened and consumed me so quickly?

Come back, my friend! The form of our love
is not a created form.

Nothing can help me but that beauty.
There was a dawn I remember

when my soul heard something
from your soul. I drank water

from your spring and felt
the current take me.

Each Note

Advice doesn't help lovers!
They're not the kind of mountain stream
you can build a dam across.

An intellectual doesn't know
what the drunk is feeling!

Don't try to figure
what those lost inside love
will do next!

Someone in charge would give up all his power,
if he caught one whiff of the wine-musk
from the room where the lovers
are doing who-knows-what!

One of them tries to dig a hole through a mountain.
One flees from academic honors.
One laughs at famous mustaches!

Life freezes if it doesn't get a taste
of this almond cake.
       The stars come up spinning

every night, bewildered in love.

                                    They'd grow tired
with that revolving, if they weren't.

                                    They'd say,
'How long do we have to *do* this!'

God picks up the reed-flute world and blows.
Each note is a need coming through one of us,
a passion, a longing-pain.

                                      Remember the lips
where the wind-breath originated,
and let your note be clear.
Don't try to end it.
Be your note.
I'll show you how it's enough.

Go up on the roof at night
in this city of the soul.

Let *everyone* climb on their roofs
and sing their notes!

Sing loud!

Music Master

You that love lovers,
this is your home. Welcome!

In the midst of making form, love
made this form that melts form,
with love for the door,
soul the vestibule.

Watch the dust grains moving
in the light near the window.

Their dance is our dance.

We rarely hear the inward music,
but we're all dancing to it nevertheless,

directed by the one who teaches us,
the pure joy of the sun,
our music master.

★

When I am with you, we stay up all night.
When you're not here, I can't go to sleep.

Praise God for these two insomnias!
And the difference between them.

★

The minute I heard my first love story
I started looking for you, not knowing
how blind that was.

Lovers don't finally meet somewhere.
They're in each other all along.

★

We are the mirror as well as the face in it.
We are tasting the taste this minute
of eternity. We are pain
and what cures pain, both. We are
the sweet cold water and the jar that pours.

★

I want to hold you close like a lute,
so we can cry out with loving.

You would rather throw stones at a mirror?
I am your mirror, and here are the stones.

Meadowsounds

We've come again to that knee of seacoast
no ocean can reach.

Tie together all human intellects.
They won't stretch to here.

The sky bares its neck so beautifully,
but gets no kiss. Only a taste.

This is the food that everyone wants,
wandering the wilderness, 'Please give us
your manna and quail.'

We're here again with the beloved.
This air, a shout. These meadowsounds,
an astonishing myth.

We've come into the presence of the one
who was never apart from us.

When the waterbag is filling, you know
the water carrier's here!

The bag leans lovingly against your shoulder.
'Without you I have no knowledge,
no way to touch anyone.'

When someone chews sugarcane,
he's wanting this sweetness.

Inside this globe the soul roars like thunder.
And now silence, my strict tutor.

I won't try to talk about Shams.
Language cannot touch that presence.

No Room for Form

On the night when you cross the street
from your shop and your house
to the cemetery,

you'll hear me hailing you from inside
the open grave, and you'll realize
how we've always been together.

I am the clear consciousness-core
of your being, the same in
ecstasy as in self-hating fatigue.

That night, when you escape the fear of snakebite
and all irritation with the ants, you'll hear
my familiar voice, see the candle being lit,
smell the incense, the surprise meal fixed
by the lover inside all your other lovers.

This heart-tumult is my signal
to you igniting in the tomb.

So don't fuss with the shroud
and the graveyard road dust.

Those get ripped open and washed away
in the music of our finally meeting.

And don't look for me in a human shape.
I am inside your looking. No room
for form with love this strong.

Beat the drum and let the poets speak.
This is a day of purification for those who
are already mature and initiated into what love is.

No need to wait until we die!
There's more to want here than money
and being famous and bites of roasted meat.

Now, what shall we call this new sort of gazing-house
that has opened in our town where people sit
quietly and pour out their glancing
like light, like answering?

Dying, Laughing

A lover was telling his beloved
how much he loved her, how faithful
he had been, how self-sacrificing, getting up
at dawn every morning, fasting, giving up
wealth and strength and fame,
all for her.

There was a fire in him.
He didn't know where it came from,
but it made him weep and melt like a candle.

'You've done well,' she said, 'but listen to me.
All this is the decor of love, the branches
and leaves and blossoms. You must live
at the root to be a true lover.'
                                        'Where is that!
Tell me!'
          'You've done the outward acts,
but you haven't died. You must die.'

When he heard that, he lay back on the ground
laughing, and died. He opened like a rose
that drops to the ground and died laughing.

That laughter was his freedom,
and his gift to the eternal.

As moonlight shines back at the sun,
he heard the call to come home, and went.

When light returns to its source,
it takes nothing
of what it has illuminated.

It may have shone on a garbage dump, or a garden,
or in the center of a human eye. No matter.

It goes, and when it does,
the open plain becomes passionately desolate,
wanting it back.

A Dove in the Eaves

When I press my hand to my chest,
it is your chest.

And now you're scratching my head!

Sometimes you put me in the herd
with your other camels.

Sometimes you place me at the front of the troops
as the commander. Sometimes you wet me
with your mouth like you do your seal-ring
just before you plant your power.

Sometimes you round me
into a simple door knocker.

You take blood and make sperm.
You take sperm and create an animal.
You use the animal to evolve intelligence.
Life keeps leading to more life.

You drive me away gently
as a flute song does a dove
from the eaves.

With the same song
you call me back.

You push me out on many journeys;
then you anchor me with no motion at all.

I am water. I am the thorn
that catches someone's clothing.

I don't care about marvelous sights!
I only want to be in your presence.

There's nothing to *believe*.
Only when I quit believing in myself
did I come into this beauty.

I saw your blade and burned my shield!
I flew on six hundred pairs of wings like Gabriel.
But now that I'm here, what do I need wings for?

Day and night I guarded the pearl of my soul.
Now in this ocean of pearling currents,
I've lost track of which was mine.

There is no way to describe you.
Say the end of this so strongly
that I will ride up over
my own commotion.

★

We have this way of talking, and we have another.
Apart from what we wish and what we fear may
    happen,

we are alive with other life, as clear stones
take form in the mountain.

★

This piece of food cannot be eaten,
nor this bit of wisdom found by looking.
There is a secret core in everyone not
even Gabriel can know by trying to know.

★

In the slaughterhouse of love, they kill
only the best, none of the weak or deformed.
Don't run away from this dying.
Whoever's not killed for love is dead meat.

Sublime Generosity

I was dead, then alive.
Weeping, then laughing.

The power of love came into me,
and I became fierce like a lion,
then tender like the evening star.

He said, 'You're not mad enough.
You don't belong in this house.'

I went wild and had to be tied up.
He said, 'Still not wild enough
to stay with us!'

I broke through another layer
into joyfulness.

He said, 'It's not enough.'
I died.

He said, 'You're a clever little man,
full of fantasy and doubting.'

I plucked out my feathers and became a fool.
He said, 'Now you're the candle
for this assembly.'

But I'm no candle. Look!
I'm scattered smoke.

He said, 'You are the sheikh, the guide.'
But I'm not a teacher. I have no power.

He said, 'You already have wings.
I cannot give you wings.'

But I wanted *his* wings.
I felt like some flightless chicken.

Then new events said to me,
'Don't move. A sublime generosity is
coming toward you.'

And old love said, 'Stay with me.'

I said, 'I will.'

You are the fountain of the sun's light.
I am a willow shadow on the ground.
You make my raggedness silky.

The soul at dawn is like darkened water
that slowly begins to say *Thank you, thank you.*

Then at sunset, again, Venus gradually
changes into the moon and then the whole nightsky.

This comes of smiling back
at your smile.

The chess master says nothing,
other than moving the silent chess piece.

That I am part of the ploys
of this game makes me
amazingly happy.

Unmarked Boxes

Don't grieve. Anything you lose comes round
in another form. The child weaned from mother's milk
now drinks wine and honey mixed.

God's joy moves from unmarked box to unmarked box,
from cell to cell. As rainwater, down into flowerbed.
As roses, up from ground.
Now it looks like a plate of rice and fish,
now a cliff covered with vines,
now a horse being saddled.
It hides within these,
till one day it cracks them open.

Part of the self leaves the body when we sleep
and changes shape. You might say, 'Last night
I was a cypress tree, a small bed of tulips,
a field of grapevines.' Then the phantasm goes away.
You're back in the room.
I don't want to make anyone fearful.
Hear what's behind what I say.

Tatatumtum tatum tatadum.
There's the light gold of wheat in the sun
and the gold of bread made from that wheat.
I have neither. I'm only talking about them,

as a town in the desert looks up
at stars on a clear night.

Dissolver of Sugar

Dissolver of sugar, dissolve me,
if this is the time.
Do it gently with a touch of a hand, or a look.
Every morning I wait at dawn. That's when
it's happened before. Or do it suddenly
like an execution. How else
can I get ready for death?

You breathe without a body like a spark.
You grieve, and I begin to feel lighter.
You keep me away with your arm,
but the keeping away is pulling me in.

*

Pale sunlight,
pale the wall.

Love moves away.
The light changes.

I need more grace
than I thought.

The Fragile Vial

I need a mouth as wide as the sky
to say the nature of a True Person, language
as large as longing.

The fragile vial inside me often breaks.
No wonder I go mad and disappear for three days
every month with the moon.

For anyone in love with you,
it's always these invisible days.

I've lost the thread of the story I was telling.
My elephant roams his dream of Hindustan again.
Narrative, poetics, destroyed, my body,
a dissolving, a return.

Friend, I've shrunk to a hair trying to say your story.
Would you tell mine?
I've made up so many love stories.
Now I feel fictional.
Tell *me*!
The truth is, you are speaking, not me.
I am Sinai, and you are Moses walking there.
This poetry is an echo of what you say.

A piece of land can't speak, or know anything!
Or if it can, only within limits.

The body is a device to calculate
the astronomy of the spirit.
Look through that astrolabe
and become oceanic.

Why this distracted talk?
It's not my fault I rave.
You did this.
Do you approve of my love-madness?

Say yes.
What language will you say it in, Arabic or Persian,
or what? Once again, I must be tied up.
Bring the curly ropes of your hair.
                         Now I remember the story.
A True Man stares at his old shoes
and sheepskin jacket. Every day he goes up
to his attic to look at his work-shoes and worn-out coat.
This is his wisdom, to remember the original clay
and not get drunk with ego and arrogance.

To visit those shoes and jacket
is praise.

The Absolute works with nothing.
The workshop, the materials
are what does not exist.

Try and be a sheet of paper with nothing on it.
Be a spot of ground where nothing is growing,
where something might be planted,
a seed, possibly, from the Absolute.

Enough Words?

How does a part of the world leave the world?
How can wetness leave water?

Don't try to put out a fire
by throwing on more fire!
Don't wash a wound with blood!

No matter how fast you run,
your shadow more than keeps up.
Sometimes, it's in front!

Only full, overhead sun
diminishes your shadow.

But that shadow has been serving you!
What hurts you, blesses you.
Darkness is your candle.
Your boundaries are your quest.

I can explain this, but it would break
the glass cover on your heart,
and there's no fixing that.

You must have shadow and light source both.
Listen, and lay your head under the tree of awe.

When from that tree, feathers and wings sprout
on you, be quieter than a dove.
Don't open your mouth for even a *cooooooo*.

When a frog slips into the water, the snake
cannot get it. Then the frog climbs back out
and croaks, and the snake moves toward him again.

Even if the frog learned to hiss, still the snake
would hear through the hiss the information
he needed, the frog voice underneath.

But if the frog could be completely silent,
then the snake would go back to sleeping,
and the frog could reach the barley.

The soul lives there in the silent breath.

And that grain of barley is such that,
when you put it in the ground,
it grows.
        Are these enough words,
or shall I squeeze more juice from this?
Who am I, my friend?

My Worst Habit

My worst habit is I get so tired of winter
I become a torture to those I'm with.

If you're not here, nothing grows.
I lack clarity. My words
tangle and knot up.

How to cure bad water? Send it back to the river.
How to cure bad habits? Send me back to you.

When water gets caught in habitual whirlpools,
dig a way out through the bottom
to the ocean. There is a secret medicine
given only to those who hurt so hard
they can't hope.

The hopers would feel slighted if they knew.

Look as long as you can at the friend you love,
no matter whether that friend is moving away
    from you
or coming back toward you.

★

Don't let your throat tighten
with fear. Take sips of breath
all day and night, before death
closes your mouth.

Dervish at the Door

A dervish knocked at a house
to ask for a piece of dry bread,
or moist, it didn't matter.

'This is not a bakery,' said the owner.

'Might you have a bit of gristle then?'

'Does this look like a butchershop?'

'A little flour?'

'Do you hear a grinding stone?'

'Some water?'

'This is not a well.'

Whatever the dervish asked for,
the man made some tired joke
and refused to give him anything.

Finally the dervish ran in the house,
lifted his robe, and squatted
as though to take a shit.

'Hey, hey!'

'Quiet, you sad man. A deserted place
is a fine spot to relieve oneself,
and since there's no living thing here,
or means of living, it needs fertilizing.'

The dervish began his own list
of questions and answers.

'What kind of bird are you? Not a falcon,
trained for the royal hand. Not a peacock,
painted with everyone's eyes. Not a parrot,
that talks for sugar cubes. Not a nightingale,
that sings like someone in love.

Not a hoopoe bringing messages to Solomon,
or a stork that builds on a cliffside.

What exactly do you do?
You are no known species.

You haggle and make jokes
to keep what you own for yourself.

You have forgotten the One
who doesn't care about ownership,
who doesn't try to turn a profit
from every human exchange.'

Tending Two Shops

Don't run around this world
looking for a hole to hide in.

There are wild beasts in *every* cave!
If you live with mice,
the cat claws will find you.

The only real rest comes
when you're alone with God.

Live in the nowhere that you came from,
even though you have an address here.

That's why you see things in two ways.
Sometimes you look at a person
and see a cynical snake.

Someone else sees a joyful lover,
and you're both right!

Everyone is half and half,
like the black and white ox.

Joseph looked ugly to his brothers,
and most handsome to his father.

You have eyes that see from that nowhere,
and eyes that judge distances,
how high and how low.

You own two shops,
and you run back and forth.

Try to close the one that's a fearful trap,
getting always smaller. Checkmate,
this way. Checkmate that.

Keep open the shop
where you're not selling fishhooks anymore.
You are the free-swimming fish.

*

Think that you're gliding out from the face of a cliff
like an eagle. Think you're walking
like a tiger walks by himself in the forest.
You're most handsome when you're after food.

Spend less time with nightingales and peacocks.
One is just a voice, the other just a color.

Hallaj

Hallaj said what he said and went to the origin
through the hole in the scaffold.

I cut a cap's worth of cloth from his robe,
and it swamped over me from head to foot.

Years ago, I broke a bunch of roses
from the top of his wall. A thorn from that
is still in my palm, working deeper.

From Hallaj, I learned to hunt lions,
but I became something hungrier than a lion.

I was a frisky colt. He broke me
with a quiet hand on the side of my head.

A person comes to him naked. It's cold.
There's a fur coat floating in the river.

'Jump in and get it,' he says.
You dive in. You reach for the coat.
It reaches for you.

It's a live bear that has fallen in upstream,
drifting with the current.

'How long does it take!' Hallaj yells from the bank.
'Don't wait,' you answer. 'This coat
has decided to wear me home!'

A little part of a story, a hint.
Do you need long sermons on Hallaj!

Wax

When I see you and how you are,
I close my eyes to the other.
For your Solomon's seal I become wax
throughout my body. I wait to be light.
I give up opinions on all matters.
I become the reed flute for your breath.

You were inside my hand.
I kept reaching around for something.
I was inside your hand, but I kept asking questions
of those who know very little.

I must have been incredibly simple or drunk or insane
to sneak into my own house and steal money,
to climb over the fence and take my own vegetables.
But no more. I've gotten free of that ignorant fist
that was pinching and twisting my secret self.

The universe and the light of the stars come
    through me.
I am the crescent moon put up
over the gate to the festival.

Of Being Woven

'The way is full of genuine sacrifice.

The thickets blocking the path are anything
that keeps you from that, any fear
that you may be broken to bits like a glass bottle.
This road demands courage and stamina,
yet it's full of footprints! Who *are*
these companions? They are rungs
in your ladder. Use them!
With company you quicken your ascent.

You may be happy enough going along,
but with others you'll get farther, and faster.

Someone who goes cheerfully by himself
to the customs house to pay his traveler's tax
will go even more lightheartedly
when friends are with him.

Every prophet sought out companions.
A wall standing alone is useless,
but put three or four walls together,
and they'll support a roof and keep
the grain dry and safe.

When ink joins with a pen, then the blank paper
can say something. Rushes and reeds must be *woven*
to be useful as a mat. If they weren't interlaced,
the wind would blow them away.

                                        Like that, God paired up
creatures, and gave them friendship.'

This is how the fowler and the bird were arguing
about hermitic living and Islam.

It's a prolonged debate.
Husam, shorten their controversy.
Make the *Mathnawi* more nimble and less lumbering.
Agile sounds are more appealing to the heart's ear.

Elephant in the Dark

Some Hindus have an elephant to show.
No one here has ever seen an elephant.
They bring it at night to a dark room.

One by one, we go in the dark and come out
saying how we experience the animal.

One of us happens to touch the trunk.
'A water-pipe kind of creature.'

Another, the ear. 'A very strong, always moving
back and forth, fan-animal.'

Another, the leg. 'I find it still,
like a column on a temple.'

Another touches the curved back.
'A leathery throne.'

Another, the cleverest, feels the tusk.
'A rounded sword made of porcelain.'
He's proud of his description.

Each of us touches one place
and understands the whole in that way.

The palm and the fingers feeling in the dark are
how the senses explore the reality of the elephant.

If each of us held a candle there,
and if we went in together,
we could see it.

The Waterwheel

Stay together, friends.
Don't scatter and sleep.

Our friendship is made
of being awake.

The waterwheel accepts water
and turns and gives it away,
weeping.

That way it stays in the garden,
whereas another roundness rolls
through a dry riverbed looking
for what it thinks it wants.

Stay here, quivering with each moment
like a drop of mercury.

This We Have Now

This we have now
is not imagination.

This is not
grief or joy.

Not a judging state,
or an elation,
or sadness.

Those come
and go.

This is the presence
that doesn't.

It's dawn, Husam,
here in the splendor of coral,
inside the Friend, the simple truth
of what Hallaj said.

What else could human beings want?

When grapes turn to wine,
they're wanting
this.

When the nightsky pours by,
it's really a crowd of beggars,
and they all want some of this!

This
that we are now
created the body, cell by cell,
like bees building a honeycomb.

The human body and the universe
grew from this, not this
from the universe and the human body.

The Seed Market

Can you find another market like this?

Where,
with your one rose
you can buy hundreds of rose gardens?

Where,
for one seed
you get a whole wilderness?

For one weak breath,
the divine wind?

You've been fearful
of being absorbed in the ground,
or drawn up by the air.

Now, your waterbead lets go
and drops into the ocean,
where it came from.

It no longer has the form it had,
but it's still water.
The essence is the same.

This giving up is not a repenting.
It's a deep honoring of yourself.

When the ocean comes to you as a lover,
marry, at once, quickly,
for God's sake!

Don't postpone it!
Existence has no better gift.

No amount of searching
will find this.

A perfect falcon, for no reason,
has landed on your shoulder,
and become yours.

The Worm's Waking

This is how a human being can change:

there's a worm addicted to eating
grape leaves.
               Suddenly, he wakes up,
call it grace, whatever, something
wakes him, and he's no longer
a worm.
           He's the entire vineyard,
and the orchard too, the fruit, the trunks,
a growing wisdom and joy
that doesn't need
to devour.

PENGUIN ARCHIVE

H. G. Wells *The Time Machine*
M. R. James *The Stalls of Barchester Cathedral*
Jane Austen *The History of England by a Partial, Prejudiced and Ignorant Historian*
Edgar Allan Poe *Hop-Frog*
Virginia Woolf *The New Dress*
Antoine de Saint-Exupéry *Night Flight*
Oscar Wilde *A Poet Can Survive Everything But a Misprint*
George Orwell *Can Socialists be Happy?*
Dorothy Parker *Horsie*
D. H. Lawrence *Odour of Chrysanthemums*
Homer *The Wrath of Achilles*
Emily Brontë *No Coward Soul Is Mine*
Romain Gary *Lady L.*
Charles Dickens *The Chimes*
Dante *Hell*
Georges Simenon *Stan the Killer*
F. Scott Fitzgerald *The Rich Boy*
Katherine Mansfield *A Dill Pickle*
Fyodor Dostoyevsky *The Dream of a Ridiculous Man*

Franz Kafka *A Hunger-Artist*
Leo Tolstoy *Family Happiness*
Karen Blixen *The Dreaming Child*
Federico García Lorca *Cicada!*
Vladimir Nabokov *Revenge*
Albert Camus *A Short Guide to Towns Without a Past*
Muriel Spark *The Driver's Seat*
Carson McCullers *Reflections in a Golden Eye*
Wu Cheng'en *Monkey King Makes Havoc in Heaven*
Friedrich Nietzsche *Ecce Homo*
Laurie Lee *A Moment of War*
Roald Dahl *Lamb to the Slaughter*
Frank O'Connor *The Genius*
James Baldwin *The Fire Next Time*
Hermann Hesse *Strange News from Another Planet*
Gertrude Stein *Paris France*
Seneca *Why I am a Stoic*
Snorri Sturluson *The Prose Edda*
Elizabeth Gaskell *Lois the Witch*
Sei Shōnagon *A Lady in Kyoto*
Yasunari Kawabata *Thousand Cranes*
Jack Kerouac *Tristessa*
Arthur Schnitzler *A Confirmed Bachelor*
Chester Himes *All God's Chillun Got Pride*

Bram Stoker *The Burial of the Rats*
Czesław Miłosz *Rescue*
Hans Christian Andersen *The Emperor's New Clothes*
Bohumil Hrabal *Closely Watched Trains*
Italo Calvino *Under the Jaguar Sun*
Stanislaw Lem *The Seventh Voyage*
Shirley Jackson *The Daemon Lover*
Stefan Zweig *Chess*
Kate Chopin *The Story of an Hour*
Allen Ginsberg *Sunflower Sutra*
Rabindranath Tagore *The Broken Nest*
Søren Kierkegaard *The Seducer's Diary*
Mary Shelley *Transformation*
Nikolai Leskov *Night Owls*
Willa Cather *A Lost Lady*
Emilia Pardo Bazán *The Lady Bandit*
W. B. Yeats *Sailing to Byzantium*
Margaret Cavendish *The Blazing World*
Lafcadio Hearn *Some Japanese Ghosts*
Sarah Orne Jewett *The Country of the Pointed Firs*
Vincent van Gogh *For Art and for Life*
Dylan Thomas *Do Not Go Gentle Into That Good Night*
Mikhail Bulgakov *A Dog's Heart*
Saadat Hasan Manto *The Price of Freedom*

Gérard de Nerval *October Nights*
Rumi *Where Everything is Music*
H. P. Lovecraft *The Shadow Out of Time*
Christina Rossetti *To Read and Dream*
Dambudzo Marechera *The House of Hunger*
Andy Warhol *Beauty*
Maurice Leblanc *The Escape of Arsène Lupin*
Eileen Chang *Jasmine Tea*
Irmgard Keun *After Midnight*
Walter Benjamin *Unpacking My Library*
Epictetus *Whatever is Rational is Tolerable*
Ota Pavel *How I Came to Know Fish*
César Aira *An Episode in the Life of a Landscape Painter*
Hafez *I am a Bird from Paradise*
Clarice Lispector *The Burned Sinner and the Harmonious Angels*
Maryse Condé *Tales from the Heart*
Audre Lorde *Coal*
Mary Gaitskill *Secretary*
Tove Ditlevsen *The Umbrella*
June Jordan *Passion*
Antonio Tabucchi *Requiem*
Alexander Lernet-Holenia *Baron Bagge*
Wang Xiaobo *The Maverick Pig*